William Butler Yeats

The Wind among the Reeds

Outlook

William Butler Yeats

The Wind among the Reeds

1. Auflage | ISBN: 978-3-73261-870-5

Erscheinungsort: Paderborn, Deutschland

Erscheinungsjahr: 2018

Outlook Verlag GmbH, Paderborn.

Reproduction of the original.

William Butler Yeats

The Wind among the Reeds

Outlook

The WIND AMONG THE REEDS

By

WILLIAM BUTLER YEATS

LONDON · ELKIN MATHEWS
VIGO STREET · W · MDCCCCIII
FOURTH EDITION.

THE HOSTING OF THE SIDHE

The host is riding from Knocknarea
And over the grave of Clooth-na-bare;
Caolte tossing his burning hair
And Niamh calling *Away, come away:*
Empty your heart of its mortal dream.
The winds awaken, the leaves whirl round,
Our cheeks are pale, our hair is unbound,
Our breasts are heaving, our eyes are a-gleam,
Our arms are waving, our lips are apart;
And if any gaze on our rushing band,
We come between him and the deed of his hand,
We come between him and the hope of his heart.
The host is rushing 'twixt night and day,
And where is there hope or deed as fair?
Caolte tossing his burning hair,
And Niamh calling *Away, come away.*

THE EVERLASTING VOICES

O sweet everlasting Voices be still;
Go to the guards of the heavenly fold
And bid them wander obeying your will
Flame under flame, till Time be no more;
Have you not heard that our hearts are old,
That you call in birds, in wind on the hill,
In shaken boughs, in tide on the shore?
O sweet everlasting Voices be still.

THE MOODS

Time drops in decay,
Like a candle burnt out,
And the mountains and woods
Have their day, have their day;
What one in the rout
Of the fire-born moods,
Has fallen away?

AEDH TELLS OF THE ROSE IN HIS HEART

All things uncomely and broken, all things worn out and old,
The cry of a child by the roadway, the creak of a lumbering cart,
The heavy steps of the ploughman, splashing the wintry mould,
Are wronging your image that blossoms a rose in the deeps of my heart.

The wrong of unshapely things is a wrong too great to be told;
I hunger to build them anew and sit on a green knoll apart,
With the earth and the sky and the water, remade, like a casket of gold
For my dreams of your image that blossoms a rose in the deeps of my heart.

THE HOST OF THE AIR

O'Driscoll drove with a song,
The wild duck and the drake,
From the tall and the tufted reeds
Of the drear Hart Lake.

And he saw how the reeds grew dark
At the coming of night tide,
And dreamed of the long dim hair
Of Bridget his bride.

He heard while he sang and dreamed
A piper piping away,
And never was piping so sad,
And never was piping so gay.

And he saw young men and young girls
Who danced on a level place
And Bridget his bride among them,
With a sad and a gay face.

The dancers crowded about him,
And many a sweet thing said,
And a young man brought him red wine
And a young girl white bread.

But Bridget drew him by the sleeve,
Away from the merry bands,
To old men playing at cards
With a twinkling of ancient hands.

The bread and the wine had a doom,
For these were the host of the air;
He sat and played in a dream
Of her long dim hair.

He played with the merry old men
And thought not of evil chance,
Until one bore Bridget his bride
Away from the merry dance.

He bore her away in his arms,
The handsomest young man there,
And his neck and his breast and his arms

Were drowned in her long dim hair.

O'Driscoll scattered the cards
And out of his dream awoke:
Old men and young men and young girls
Were gone like a drifting smoke;

But he heard high up in the air
A piper piping away,
And never was piping so sad,
And never was piping so gay.

BREASAL THE FISHERMAN

Although you hide in the ebb and flow
Of the pale tide when the moon has set,
The people of coming days will know
About the casting out of my net,
And how you have leaped times out ofmind
Over the little silver cords,
And think that you were hard and unkind,
And blame you with many bitter words.

A CRADLE SONG

The Danann children laugh, in cradles of wrought gold,
And clap their hands together, and half close their eyes,
For they will ride the North when the ger-eagle flies,
With heavy whitening wings, and a heart fallen cold:
I kiss my wailing child and press it to my breast, And
hear the narrow graves calling my child and me.
Desolate winds that cry over the wandering sea;
Desolate winds that hover in the flaming West;
Desolate winds that beat the doors of Heaven, and beat
The doors of Hell and blow there many a whimpering ghost;
O heart the winds have shaken; the unappeasable host
Is comelier than candles before Maurya's feet.

INTO THE TWILIGHT

Out-worn heart, in a time out-worn,
Come clear of the nets of wrong and right;
Laugh heart again in the gray twilight,
Sigh, heart, again in the dew of the morn.

Your mother Eire is always young,
Dew ever shining and twilight gray;
Though hope fall from you and love decay,
Burning in fires of a slanderous tongue.

Come, heart, where hill is heaped upon hill:
For there the mystical brotherhood
Of sun and moon and hollow and wood
And river and stream work out their will;
And God stands winding His lonely horn,
And time and the world are ever in flight;
And love is less kind than the gray twilight,
And hope is less dear than the dew of the morn.

THE SONG OF WANDERING AENGUS

I went out to the hazel wood,
Because a fire was in my head,
And cut and peeled a hazel wand,
And hooked a berry to a thread;
And when white moths were on the wing,
And moth-like stars were flickering out,
I dropped the berry in a stream
And caught a little silver trout.

When I had laid it on the floor
I went to blow the fire a-flame,
But something rustled on the floor,
And someone called me by my name:
It had become a glimmering girl
With apple blossom in her hair
Who called me by my name and ran
And faded through the brightening air.

Though I am old with wandering
Through hollow lands and hilly lands,
I will find out where she has gone,
And kiss her lips and take her hands;
And walk among long dappled grass,
And pluck till time and times are done,
The silver apples of the moon,
The golden apples of the sun.

THE SONG OF THE OLD MOTHER

I rise in the dawn, and I kneel and blow
Till the seed of the fire flicker and glow;
And then I must scrub and bake and sweep
Till stars are beginning to blink and peep;
And the young lie long and dream in their bed
Of the matching of ribbons for bosom and head,
And their day goes over in idleness,
And they sigh if the wind but lift a tress:
While I must work because I am old,
And the seed of the fire gets feeble and cold.

THE FIDDLER OF DOONEY

When I play on my fiddle in Dooney,
Folk dance like a wave of the sea;
My cousin is priest in Kilvarnet,
My brother in Moharabuiee.

I passed my brother and cousin:
They read in their books of prayer;
I read in my book of songs
I bought at the Sligo fair.

When we come at the end of time,
To Peter sitting in state,
He will smile on the three old spirits,
But call me first through the gate;

For the good are always the merry,
Save by an evil chance,
And the merry love the fiddle
And the merry love to dance:

And when the folk there spy me,
They will all come up to me,
With 'Here is the fiddler of Dooney!'
And dance like a wave of the sea.

THE HEART OF THE WOMAN

O what to me the little room
That was brimmed up with prayer and rest;
He bade me out into the gloom,
And my breast lies upon his breast.

O what to me my mother's care,
The house where I was safe and warm;
The shadowy blossom of my hair
Will hide us from the bitter storm.

O hiding hair and dewy eyes,
I am no more with life and death,
My heart upon his warm heart lies,
My breath is mixed into his breath.

AEDH LAMENTS THE LOSS OF LOVE

Pale brows, still hands and dim hair,
I had a beautiful friend
And dreamed that the old despair
Would end in love in the end:
She looked in my heart one day
And saw your image was there;
She has gone weeping away.

MONGAN LAMENTS THE CHANGE THAT HAS COME UPON HIM AND HIS BELOVED

Do you not hear me calling, white deer with no horns!
I have been changed to a hound with one red ear;
I have been in the Path of Stones and the Wood of Thorns,
For somebody hid hatred and hope and desire and fear
Under my feet that they follow you night and day.
A man with a hazel wand came without sound;
He changed me suddenly; I was looking another way;
And now my calling is but the calling of a hound;
And Time and Birth and Change are hurrying by.
I would that the boar without bristles had come from the West
And had rooted the sun and moon and stars out of the sky
And lay in the darkness, grunting, and turning to his rest.

MICHAEL ROBARTES BIDS HIS BELOVED BE AT PEACE

I hear the Shadowy Horses, their long manes a-shake,
Their hoofs heavy with tumult, their eyes glimmering white;
The North unfolds above them clinging, creeping night,
The East her hidden joy before the morning break,
The West weeps in pale dew and sighs passing away,
The South is pouring down roses of crimson fire:
O vanity of Sleep, Hope, Dream, endless Desire,
The Horses of Disaster plunge in the heavy clay:
Beloved, let your eyes half close, and your heart beat
Over my heart, and your hair fall over my breast,
Drowning love's lonely hour in deep twilight of rest,
And hiding their tossing manes and their tumultuous feet.

HANRAHAN REPROVES THE CURLEW

O, curlew, cry no more in the air,
Or only to the waters in the West;
Because your crying brings to my mind
Passion-dimmed eyes and long heavy hair
That was shaken out over my breast:
There is enough evil in the crying ofwind.

MICHAEL ROBARTES REMEMBERS
FORGOTTEN BEAUTY

When my arms wrap you round I press
My heart upon the loveliness
That has long faded from the world;
The jewelled crowns that kings have hurled
In shadowy pools, when armies fled;
The love-tales wove with silken thread
By dreaming ladies upon cloth
That has made fat the murderous moth;
The roses that of old time were
Woven by ladies in their hair,
The dew-cold lilies ladies bore
Through many a sacred corridor
Where such gray clouds of incense rose
That only the gods' eyes did not close:
For that pale breast and lingering hand
Come from a more dream-heavy land,
A more dream-heavy hour than this;
And when you sigh from kiss to kiss
I hear white Beauty sighing, too,
For hours when all must fade like dew
But flame on flame, deep under deep,
Throne over throne, where in half sleep
Their swords upon their iron knees
Brood her high lonely mysteries.

A POET TO HIS BELOVED

I bring you with reverent hands
The books of my numberless dreams;
White woman that passion has worn
As the tide wears the dove-gray sands,
And with heart more old than the horn
That is brimmed from the pale fire of time:
White woman with numberless dreams
I bring you my passionate rhyme.

AEDH GIVES HIS BELOVED CERTAIN RHYMES

Fasten your hair with a golden pin,
And bind up every wandering tress;
I bade my heart build these poor rhymes:
It worked at them, day out, day in,
Building a sorrowful loveliness
Out of the battles of old times.

You need but lift a pearl-pale hand,
And bind up your long hair and sigh;
And all men's hearts must burn and beat;
And candle-like foam on the dim sand,
And stars climbing the dew-dropping sky,
Live but to light your passing feet.

TO MY HEART, BIDDING IT HAVE NO FEAR

Be you still, be you still, trembling heart;
Remember the wisdom out of the old days:
Him who trembles before the flame and the flood,
And the winds that blow through the starry ways,
Let the starry winds and the flame and the flood
Cover over and hide, for he has no part
With the proud, majestical multitude.

THE CAP AND BELLS

The jester walked in the garden:
The garden had fallen still;
He bade his soul rise upward
And stand on her window-sill.

It rose in a straight blue garment,
When owls began to call:
It had grown wise-tongued by thinking
Of a quiet and light footfall;

But the young queen would not listen;
She rose in her pale night gown;
She drew in the heavy casement
And pushed the latches down.

He bade his heart go to her,
When the owls called out no more;
In a red and quivering garment
It sang to her through the door.

It had grown sweet-tongued by dreaming,
Of a flutter of flower-like hair;
But she took up her fan from the table
And waved it off on the air.

'I have cap and bells,' he pondered,
'I will send them to her and die;'
And when the morning whitened
He left them where she went by.

She laid them upon her bosom,
Under a cloud of her hair,
And her red lips sang them a love song:
Till stars grew out of the air.

She opened her door and her window,
And the heart and the soul came through,
To her right hand came the red one,
To her left hand came the blue.

They set up a noise like crickets,
A chattering wise and sweet,
And her hair was a folded flower

And the quiet of love in her feet.

THE VALLEY OF THE BLACK PIG

The dews drop slowly and dreams gather: unknown spears
Suddenly hurtle before my dream-awakened eyes,
And then the clash of fallen horsemen and the cries
Of unknown perishing armies beat about my ears.
We who still labour by the cromlec on the shore,
The grey cairn on the hill, when day sinks drowned in dew,
Being weary of the world's empires, bow down to you
Master of the still stars and of the flaming door.

MICHAEL ROBARTES ASKS FORGIVENESS BECAUSE OF HIS MANY MOODS

If this importunate heart trouble your peace
With words lighter than air,
Or hopes that in mere hoping flicker and cease;
Crumple the rose in your hair;
And cover your lips with odorous twilight and say,
'O Hearts of wind-blown flame!
'O Winds, elder than changing of night and day,
'That murmuring and longing came,
'From marble cities loud with tabors of old
'In dove-gray faery lands;
'From battle banners fold upon purple fold,
'Queens wrought with glimmering hands;
'That saw young Niamh hover with love-lorn face
'Above the wandering tide;
'And lingered in the hidden desolate place,
'Where the last Phœnix died
'And wrapped the flames above his holy head;
'And still murmur and long:
'O Piteous Hearts, changing till change be dead
'In a tumultuous song:'
And cover the pale blossoms of your breast
With your dim heavy hair,
And trouble with a sigh for all things longing for rest
The odorous twilight there.

AEDH TELLS OF A VALLEY FULL OF LOVERS

I dreamed that I stood in a valley, and amid sighs,
For happy lovers passed two by two where I stood;
And I dreamed my lost love came stealthily out of the wood
With her cloud-pale eyelids falling on dream-dimmed eyes:
I cried in my dream '*O women bid the young men lay*
'*Their heads on your knees, and drown their eyes with your hair,*
'*Or remembering hers they will find no other face fair*
'*Till all the valleys of the world have been withered away.*'

AEDH TELLS OF THE PERFECT BEAUTY

O cloud-pale eyelids, dream-dimmed eyes
The poets labouring all their days
To build a perfect beauty in rhyme
Are overthrown by a woman's gaze
And by the unlabouring brood of the skies:
And therefore my heart will bow, when dew
Is dropping sleep, until God burn time,
Before the unlabouring stars and you.

AEDH HEARS THE CRY OF THE SEDGE

I wander by the edge
Of this desolate lake
Where wind cries in the sedge
Until the axle break
That keeps the stars in their round
And hands hurl in the deep
The banners of East and West
And the girdle of light is unbound,
Your breast will not lie by the breast
Of your beloved in sleep.

AEDH THINKS OF THOSE WHO HAVE SPOKEN EVIL OF HIS BELOVED

Half close your eyelids, loosen your hair,
And dream about the great and their pride;
They have spoken against you everywhere,
But weigh this song with the great and their pride;
I made it out of a mouthful of air,
Their children's children shall say they have lied.

THE BLESSED

Cumhal called out, bending his head,
Till Dathi came and stood,
With a blink in his eyes at the cave mouth,
Between the wind and the wood.

And Cumhal said, bending his knees,
'I have come by the windy way
'To gather the half of your blessedness
'And learn to pray when you pray.

'I can bring you salmon out of the streams
'And heron out of the skies.'
But Dathi folded his hands and smiled
With the secrets of God in his eyes.

And Cumhal saw like a drifting smoke
All manner of blessed souls,
Women and children, young men with books,
And old men with croziers and stoles.

'Praise God and God's mother,' Dathi said,
'For God and God's mother have sent
'The blessedest souls that walk in the world
'To fill your heart with content.'

'And which is the blessedest,' Cumhal said,
'Where all are comely and good?
'Is it these that with golden thuribles
'Are singing about the wood?'

'My eyes are blinking,' Dathi said,
'With the secrets of God halfblind,
'But I can see where the wind goes
'And follow the way of the wind;

'And blessedness goes where the wind goes,
'And when it is gone we are dead;
'I see the blessedest soul in the world
'And he nods a drunken head.

'O blessedness comes in the night and the day
'And whither the wise heart knows;
'And one has seen in the redness of wine

'The Incorruptible Rose,

'That drowsily drops faint leaves on him
'And the sweetness of desire,
'While time and the world are ebbing away
'In twilights of dew and of fire.'

THE SECRET ROSE

Far off, most secret, and inviolate Rose,
Enfold me in my hour of hours; where those
Who sought thee in the Holy Sepulchre,
Or in the wine vat, dwell beyond the stir
And tumult of defeated dreams; and deep
Among pale eyelids, heavy with the sleep
Men have named beauty. Thy great leaves enfold
The ancient beards, the helms of ruby and gold
Of the crowned Magi; and the king whose eyes
Saw the Pierced Hands and Rood of elder rise
In druid vapour and make the torches dim;
Till vain frenzy awoke and he died; and him
Who met Fand walking among flaming dew
By a gray shore where the wind never blew,
And lost the world and Emer for a kiss;
And him who drove the gods out of their liss,
And till a hundred morns had flowered red,
Feasted and wept the barrows of his dead;
And the proud dreaming king who flung the crown
And sorrow away, and calling bard and clown
Dwelt among wine-stained wanderers in deep woods;
And him who sold tillage, and house, and goods,
And sought through lands and islands numberless years,
Until he found with laughter and with tears,
A woman, of so shining loveliness,
That men threshed corn at midnight by a tress,
A little stolen tress. I, too, await
The hour of thy great wind of love and hate.
When shall the stars be blown about the sky,
Like the sparks blown out of a smithy, and die?
Surely thine hour has come, thy great wind blows,
Far off, most secret, and inviolate Rose?

HANRAHAN LAMENTS BECAUSE OF HIS WANDERINGS

O where is our Mother of Peace
Nodding her purple hood?
For the winds that awakened the stars
Are blowing through my blood.
I would that the death-pale deer
Had come through the mountain side,
And trampled the mountain away,
And drunk up the murmuring tide;
For the winds that awakened the stars
Are blowing through my blood,
And our Mother of Peace has forgotme
Under her purple hood.

THE TRAVAIL OF PASSION

When the flaming lute-thronged angelic door is wide;
When an immortal passion breathes in mortal clay;
Our hearts endure the scourge, the plaited thorns, the way
Crowded with bitter faces, the wounds in palm and side,
The hyssop-heavy sponge, the flowers by Kidron stream:
We will bend down and loosen our hair over you,
That it may drop faint perfume, and be heavy with dew,
Lilies of death-pale hope, roses of passionate dream.

THE POET PLEADS WITH HIS FRIEND FOR OLD FRIENDS

Though you are in your shining days,
Voices among the crowd
And new friends busy with your praise,
Be not unkind or proud,
But think about old friends the most:
Time's bitter flood will rise,
Your beauty perish and be lost
For all eyes but these eyes.

HANRAHAN SPEAKS TO THE LOVERS OF HIS SONGS IN COMING DAYS

O, colleens, kneeling by your altar rails long hence,
When songs I wove for my beloved hide the prayer,
And smoke from this dead heart drifts through the violet air
And covers away the smoke of myrrh and frankincense;
Bend down and pray for the great sin I wove in song,
Till Maurya of the wounded heart cry a sweet cry,
And call to my beloved and me: 'No longer fly
'Amid the hovering, piteous, penitential throng.'

AEDH PLEADS WITH THE ELEMENTAL POWERS

The Powers whose name and shape no living creature knows
Have pulled the Immortal Rose;
And though the Seven Lights bowed in their dance and wept,
The Polar Dragon slept,
His heavy rings uncoiled from glimmering deep to deep:
When will he wake from sleep?

Great Powers of falling wave and wind and windy fire,
With your harmonious choir
Encircle her I love and sing her into peace,
That my old care may cease;
Unfold your flaming wings and cover out of sight
The nets of day and night.

Dim Powers of drowsy thought, let her no longer be
Like the pale cup of the sea,
When winds have gathered and sun and moon burned dim
Above its cloudy rim;
But let a gentle silence wrought with music flow
Whither her footsteps go.

AEDH WISHES HIS BELOVED WERE DEAD

Were you but lying cold and dead,
And lights were paling out of the West,
You would come hither, and bend your head,
And I would lay my head on your breast;
And you would murmur tender words,
Forgiving me, because you were dead:
Nor would you rise and hasten away,
Though you have the will of the wildbirds,
But know your hair was bound and wound
About the stars and moon and sun:
O would beloved that you lay
Under the dock-leaves in the ground,
While lights were paling one by one.

AEDH WISHES FOR THE CLOTHS OF HEAVEN

Had I the heavens' embroidered cloths,
Enwrought with golden and silver light,
The blue and the dim and the dark cloths
Of night and light and the half light,
I would spread the cloths under your feet:
But I, being poor, have only my dreams;
I have spread my dreams under your feet;
Tread softly because you tread on my dreams.

MONGAN THINKS OF HIS PAST GREATNESS

I have drunk ale from the Country of the Young
And weep because I know all things now:
I have been a hazel tree and they hung
The Pilot Star and the Crooked Plough
Among my leaves in times out of mind:
I became a rush that horses tread:
I became a man, a hater of the wind,
Knowing one, out of all things, alone, that his head
Would not lie on the breast or his lips on the hair
Of the woman that he loves, until he dies;
Although the rushes and the fowl of the air
Cry of his love with their pitiful cries.

NOTES

THE HOSTING OF THE SIDHE.

The powerful and wealthy called the gods of ancient Ireland the Tuatha De Danaan, or the Tribes of the goddess Danu, but the poor called them, and still sometimes call them, the Sidhe, from Aes Sidhe or Sluagh Sidhe, the people of the Faery Hills, as these words are usually explained. Sidhe is also Gaelic for wind, and certainly the Sidhe have much to do with the wind. They journey in whirling winds, the winds that were called the dance of the daughters of Herodias in the Middle Ages, Herodias doubtless taking the place of some old goddess. When the country people see the leaves whirling on the road they bless themselves, because they believe the Sidhe to be passing by. They are almost always said to wear no covering upon their heads, and to let their hair stream out; and the great among them, for they have great and simple, go much upon horseback. If any one becomes too much interested in them, and sees them over much, he loses all interest in ordinary things. I shall write a great deal elsewhere about such enchanted persons, and can give but an example or two now.

A woman near Gort, in Galway, says: 'There is a boy, now, of the Cloran's; but I wouldn't for the world let them think I spoke of him; it's two years since he came from America, and since that time he never went to Mass, or to church, or to fairs, or to market, or to stand on the cross roads, or to hurling, or to nothing. And if any one comes into the house, it's into the room he'll slip, not to see them; and as to work, he has the garden dug to bits, and the whole place smeared with cow dung; and such a crop as was never seen; and the alders all plaited till they look grand. One day he went as far as the chapel; but as soon as he got to the door he turned straight round again, as if he hadn't power to pass it. I wonder he wouldn't get the priest to read a Mass for him, or something; but the crop he has is grand, and you may know well he has some to help him.' One hears many stories of the kind; and a man whose son is believed to go out riding among them at night tells me that he is careless about everything, and lies in bed until it is late in the day. A doctor believes this boy to be mad. Those that are at times 'away,' as it is called, know all things, but are afraid to speak. A countryman at Kiltartan says, 'There was one of the Lydons—John—was away for seven years, lying in his bed, but brought away at nights, and he knew everything; and one, Kearney, up in the mountains, a cousin of his own, lost two hoggets, and came and told him, and he knew the very spot where they were, and told him, and he got them back again. But *they* were vexed at that, and took away the power, so that he never knew anything again, no more than another.' This wisdom is the wisdom of the fools of the Celtic stories, that was above all the wisdom of the wise. Lomna, the fool of Fiann, had so great wisdom that his head, cut from his body, was still able to sing and prophesy; and a writer in the 'Encyclopædia Britannica' writes that Tristram, in the oldest form of the tale of Tristram and Iseult, drank wisdom, and madness the shadow of wisdom, and not love, out of the magic cup.

The great of the old times are among the Tribes of Danu, and are kings and queens among them. Caolte was a companion of Fiann; and years after his death he appeared to a king in a forest, and was a flaming man, that he might lead him in the darkness. When the king asked him who he was, he said, 'I am your candlestick.' I do not remember where I have read this story, and I have, maybe, half forgotten it. Niam was a beautiful woman of the Tribes of Danu, that led Oisin to the Country of the Young, as their country is called; I have written about her in 'The Wandering of Usheen;' and he came back, at last, to bitterness and weariness.

Knocknarea is in Sligo, and the country people say that Maeve, still a great queen of the western Sidhe, is buried in the cairn of stones upon it. I have written of Clooth-na-Bare in 'The Celtic Twilight.' She 'went all over the world, seeking a lake deep enough to drown her faery life, of which she had grown weary, leaping from hill to hill, and setting up a cairn of stones wherever her feet lighted, until, at last, she found the deepest water in the world in little Lough Ia, on the top of the bird mountain, in Sligo.' I forget, now, where I heard this story, but it may have been from a priest at Collooney. Clooth-na-Bare would mean the old woman of Bare, but is evidently a corruption of Cailleac Bare, the old woman Bare, who, under the names Bare, and Berah, and Beri, and Verah, and Dera, and Dhira, appears in the legends of many places. Mr. O'Grady found her haunting Lough Liath high up on the top of a mountain of the Fews, the Slieve Fuadh, or Slieve G-Cullain of old times, under the name of the Cailleac Buillia. He describes Lough Liath as a desolate moon-shaped lake, with made wells and sunken passages upon its borders, and beset by marsh and heather and gray boulders, and closes his 'Flight of the Eagle' with a long rhapsody upon mountain and lake, because of the heroic tales and beautiful old myths that have hung about them always. He identifies the Cailleac Buillia with that Meluchra who persuaded Fionn to go to her amid the waters of Lough Liath, and so changed him with her enchantments, that, though she had to free him because of the threats of the Fiana, his hair was ever afterwards as white as snow. To this day the Tribes of the Goddess Danu that are in the waters beckon to men, and drown them in the waters; and Bare, or Dhira, or Meluchra, or whatever name one likes the best, is, doubtless, the name of a mistress among them. Meluchra was daughter of Cullain; and Cullain Mr. O'Grady calls, upon I know not what authority, a form of Lir, the master of waters. The people of the waters have been in all ages beautiful and changeable and lascivious, or beautiful and wise and lonely, for water is everywhere the signature of the fruitfulness of the body and of the fruitfulness of dreams. The white hair of Fionn may be but another of the troubles of those that come to unearthly wisdom and earthly trouble, and the threats and violence of the Fiana against her, a different form of the threats and violence the country people use, to make the Tribes of Danu give up those that are 'away.' Bare is now often called an ugly old woman; but Dr. Joyce says that one of her old names was Aebhin, which means beautiful. Aebhen was the goddess of the tribes of northern Leinster; and the lover she had made immortal, and who loved her perfectly, left her, and put on mortality, to fight among them against the stranger, and died on the strand of Clontarf.

'Aedh,' 'Hanrahan' and 'Michael Robartes' in these Poems.

These are personages in 'The Secret Rose;' but, with the exception of some of Hanrahan's and one of Aedh's poems, the poems are not out of that book. I have used them in this book more as principles of the mind than as actual personages. It is probable that only students of the magical tradition will understand me when I say that 'Michael Robartes' is fire reflected in water, and that Hanrahan is fire blown by the wind, and that Aedh, whose name is not merely the Irish form of Hugh, but the Irish for fire, is fire burning by itself. To put it in a different way, Hanrahan is the simplicity of an imagination too changeable to gather permanent possessions, or the adoration of the shepherds; and Michael Robartes is the pride of the imagination brooding upon the greatness of its possessions, or the adoration of the Magi; while Aedh is the myrrh and frankincense that the imagination offers continually before all that it loves.

Aedh pleads with the Elemental Powers.

Mongan thinks of his past Greatness.

Aedh hears the Cry of the Sedge.

The Rose has been for many centuries a symbol of spiritual love and supreme beauty. The Count Goblet D'Alviella thinks that it was once a symbol of the sun,—itself a principal symbol of the divine nature, and the symbolic heart of things. The lotus was in some Eastern countries imagined blossoming upon the Tree of Life, as the Flower of Life, and is thus represented in Assyrian bas-reliefs. Because the Rose, the flower sacred to the Virgin Mary, and the flower that Apuleius' adventurer ate, when he was changed out of the ass's shape and received into the fellowship of Isis, is the western Flower of Life, I have imagined it growing upon the Tree of Life. I once stood beside a man in Ireland when he saw it growing there in a vision, that seemed to have rapt him out of his body. He saw the garden of Eden walled about, and on the top of a high mountain, as in certain mediæval diagrams, and after passing the Tree of Knowledge, on which grew fruit full of troubled faces, and through whose branches flowed, he was told, sap that was human souls, he came to a tall, dark tree, with little bitter fruits, and was shown a kind of stair or ladder going up through the tree, and told to go up; and near the top of the tree, a beautiful woman, like the Goddess of Life associated with the tree in Assyria, gave him a rose that seemed to have been growing upon the tree. One finds the Rose in the Irish poets, sometimes as a religious symbol, as in the phrase, 'the Rose of Friday,' meaning the Rose of austerity, in a Gaelic poem in Dr. Hyde's 'Religious Songs of Connacht;' and, I think, as a symbol of woman's beauty in the Gaelic song, 'Roseen Dubh;' and a symbol of Ireland in Mangan's adaptation of 'Roseen Dubh,' 'My Dark Rosaleen,' and in Mr. Aubrey de Vere's 'The Little Black Rose.' I do not know any evidence to prove whether this symbol came to Ireland with mediæval Christianity, or whether it has come down from Celtic times. I have read somewhere that a stone engraved with a Celtic god, who holds what looks like a rose in one hand, has been found somewhere in England; but I cannot find the reference, though I certainly made a note of it. If the Rose was really a symbol of Ireland among the Gaelic poets, and if 'Roseen Dubh' is really a political poem, as some think, one may feel pretty certain that the ancient Celts associated the Rose with Eire, or Fotla, or Banba—goddesses who gave their names to Ireland— or with some principal god or goddess, for such symbols are not suddenly adopted or invented, but come out of mythology.

I have made the Seven Lights, the constellation of the Bear, lament for the theft of the Rose, and I have made the Dragon, the constellation Draco, the guardian of the Rose, because these constellations move about the pole of the heavens, the ancient Tree of Life in many countries, and are often associated with the Tree of Life in mythology. It is this Tree of Life that I have put into the 'Song of Mongan' under its common Irish form of a hazel; and, because it had sometimes the stars for fruit, I have hung upon it 'the Crooked Plough' and the 'Pilot' star, as Gaelic-speaking Irishmen sometimes call the Bear and the North star. I have made it an axle-tree in 'Aedh hears the Cry of the Sedge,' for this was another ancient way of representing it.

The Host of the Air.

Some writers distinguish between the Sluagh Gaoith, the host of the air, and Sluagh Sidhe, the host of the Sidhe, and describe the host of the air as of a peculiar malignancy. Dr. Joyce says, 'of all the different kinds of goblins … air demons were most dreaded by the people. They lived among clouds, and mists, and rocks, and hated the human race with the utmost malignity.' A very old Arann charm, which contains the words 'Send God, by his strength, between us and the host of the Sidhe, between us and the host of the air,' seems also to distinguish among them. I am inclined, however, to think that the distinction came in with Christianity and its belief about the prince of the air, for the host of the Sidhe, as I have already explained, are closely associated with the wind.

They are said to steal brides just after their marriage, and sometimes in a blast of wind. A man in Galway says, 'At Aughanish there were two couples came to the shore to be married, and one of the newly married women was in the boat with the priest, and they going back to the island; and a sudden blast of wind came, and the priest said some blessed words that were able to save himself, but the girl was swept.'

This woman was drowned; but more often the persons who are taken 'get the touch,' as it is called, and fall into a half dream, and grow indifferent to all things, for their true life has gone out of the world, and is among the hills and the forts of the Sidhe. A faery doctor has told me that his wife 'got the touch' at her marriage because there was one of them wanted her; and the way he knew for certain was, that when he took a pitchfork out of the rafters, and told her it was a broom, she said, 'It is a broom.' She was, the truth is, in the magical sleep, to which people have given a new name lately, that makes the imagination so passive that it can be moulded by any voice in any world into any shape. A mere likeness of some old woman, or even old animal, some one or some thing the Sidhe have no longer a use for, is believed to be left instead of the person who is 'away;' this some one or some thing can, it is thought, be driven away by threats, or by violence (though I have heard country women say that violence is wrong), which perhaps awakes the soul out of the magical sleep. The story in the poem is founded on an old Gaelic ballad that was sung and translated for me by a woman at Ballisodare in County Sligo; but in the ballad the husband found the keeners keening his wife when he got to his house. She was 'swept' at once; but the Sidhe are said to value those the most whom they but cast into a half dream, which may last for years, for they need the help of a living person in most of the things they do. There are many stories of people who seem to die and be buried—though the country people will tell you it is but some one or some thing put in their place that dies and is buried—and yet are brought back afterwards. These tales are perhaps memories of true awakenings out of the magical sleep, moulded by the imagination, under the influence of a mystical doctrine which it understands too literally, into the shape of some well-known traditional tale. One does not hear them as one hears the others, from the persons who are 'away,' or from their wives or husbands; and one old man, who had often seen the Sidhe, began one of them with 'Maybe it is all vanity.'

Here is a tale that a friend of mine heard in the Burren hills, and it is a type of all:—

'There was a girl to be married, and she didn't like the man, and she cried when the day was coming, and said she wouldn't go along with him. And the mother said, "Get into the bed, then, and I'll say that you're sick." And so she did. And when the man came the mother said to him, "You can't get her, she's sick in the bed." And he looked in and said, "That's not my wife that's in the bed, it's some old hag." And the mother began to cry and to roar. And he went out and got two hampers of turf, and made a fire, that they thought he was going to burn the house down. And when the fire was kindled, "Come out now," says he, "and we'll see who you are, when I'll put you on the fire." And when she heard that, she gave one leap, and was out of the house, and they saw, then, it was an old hag she was. Well, the man asked the advice of an old woman, and she bid him go to a faery-bush that was near, and he might get some word of her. So he went there at night, and saw all sorts of grand people, and they in carriages or riding on horses, and among them he could see the girl he came to look for. So he went again to the old woman, and she said, "If you can get the three bits of blackthorn out of her hair, you'll get her again." So that night he went again, and that time he only got hold of a bit of her hair. But the old woman told him that was no use, and that he was put back now, and it might be twelve nights before he'd get her. But on the fourth night he got the third bit of blackthorn, and he took her, and she came away with him. He never told the mother he had got her; but one day she saw her at a fair, and, says she, "That's my daughter; I know her by the smile and by the laugh of her," and she with a shawl about her head. So the husband said, "You're right there, and hard I worked to get her." She spoke often of the grand things she saw underground, and how she used to have wine to drink, and to drive out in a carriage with four horses every night. And she used to be able to see her husband when he came to look for her, and she was greatly afraid he'd get a drop of the wine, for then he would have come underground and never left it again. And she was glad herself to come to earth again, and not to be left there.'

The old Gaelic literature is full of the appeals of the Tribes of the goddess

Danu to mortals whom they would bring into their country; but the song of Midher to the beautiful Etain, the wife of the king who was called Echaid the ploughman, is the type of all.

'O beautiful woman, come with me to the marvellous land where one listens to a sweet music, where one has spring flowers in one's hair, where the body is like snow from head to foot, where no one is sad or silent, where teeth are white and eyebrows are black ... cheeks red like foxglove in flower.... Ireland is beautiful, but not so beautiful as the Great Plain I call you to. The beer of Ireland is heady, but the beer of the Great Plain is much more heady. How marvellous is the country I am speaking of! Youth does not grow old there. Streams with warm flood flow there; sometimes mead, sometimes wine. Men are charming and without a blot there, and love is not forbidden there. O woman, when you come into my powerful country you will wear a crown of gold upon your head. I will give you the flesh of swine, and you will have beer and milk to drink, O beautiful woman. O beautiful woman, come with me!'

A Cradle Song.

Michael Robartes asks Forgiveness because of his many Moods.

I use the wind as a symbol of vague desires and hopes, not merely because the Sidhe are in the wind, or because the wind bloweth as it listeth, but because wind and spirit and vague desire have been associated everywhere. A highland scholar tells me that his country people use the wind in their talk and in their proverbs as I use it in my poem.

The Song of Wandering Aengus.

The Tribes of the goddess Danu can take all shapes, and those that are in the waters take often the shape of fish. A woman of Burren, in Galway, says, 'There are more of them in the sea than on the land, and they sometimes try to come over the side of the boat in the form of fishes, for they can take their choice shape.' At other times they are beautiful women; and another Galway woman says, 'Surely those things are in the sea as well as on land. My father was out fishing one night off Tyrone. And something came beside the boat that had eyes shining like candles. And then a wave came in, and a storm rose all in a minute, and whatever was in the wave, the weight of it had like to sink the boat. And then they saw that it was a woman in the sea that had the shining eyes. So my father went to the priest, and he bid him always to take a drop of holy water and a pinch of salt out in the boat with him, and nothing could harm him.'

The poem was suggested to me by a Greek folk song; but the folk belief of Greece is very like that of Ireland, and I certainly thought, when I wrote it, of Ireland, and of the spirits that are in Ireland. An old man who was cutting a quickset hedge near Gort, in Galway, said, only the other day, 'One time I was cutting timber over in Inchy, and about eight o'clock one morning, when I got there, I saw a girl picking nuts, with her hair hanging down over her shoulders; brown hair; and she had a good, clean face, and she was tall, and nothing on her head, and her dress no way gaudy, but simple. And when she felt me coming she gathered herself up, and was gone, as if the earth had swallowed her up. And I followed her, and looked for her, but I never could see her again from that day to this, never again.'

The county Galway people use the word 'clean' in its old sense of fresh and comely.

MICHAEL ROBARTES BIDS HIS BELOVED BE AT PEACE.

November, the old beginning of winter, or of the victory of the Fomor, or powers of death, and dismay, and cold, and darkness, is associated by the Irish people with the horse-shaped Púcas, who are now mischievous spirits, but were once Fomorian divinities. I think that they may have some connection with the horses of Mannannan, who reigned over the country of the dead, where the Fomorian Tethra reigned also; and the horses of Mannannan, though they could cross the land as easily as the sea, are constantly associated with the waves. Some neo-platonist, I forget who, describes the sea as a symbol of the drifting indefinite bitterness of life, and I believe there is like symbolism intended in the many Irish voyages to the islands of enchantment, or that there was, at any rate, in the mythology out of which these stories have been shaped. I follow much Irish and other mythology, and the magical tradition, in associating the North with night and sleep, and the East, the place of sunrise, with hope, and the South, the place of the sun when at its height, with passion and desire, and the West, the place of sunset, with fading and dreaming things.

MONGAN LAMENTS THE CHANGE THAT HAS COME UPON HIM AND HIS BELOVED.

HANRAHAN LAMENTS BECAUSE OF HIS WANDERINGS.

My deer and hound are properly related to the deer and hound that flicker in and out of the various tellings of the Arthurian legends, leading different knights upon adventures, and to the hounds and to the hornless deer at the beginning of, I think, all tellings of Oisin's journey to the country of the young. The hound is certainly related to the Hounds of Annwvyn or of Hades, who are white, and have red ears, and were heard, and are, perhaps, still heard by Welsh peasants following some flying thing in the night winds; and is probably related to the hounds that Irish country people believe will awake and seize the souls of the dead if you lament them too loudly or too soon, and to the hound the son of Setanta killed, on what was certainly, in the first form of the tale, a visit to the Celtic Hades. An old woman told a friend and myself that she saw what she thought were white birds, flying over an enchanted place, but found, when she got near, that they had dog's heads; and I do not doubt that my hound and these dog-headed birds are of the same family. I got my hound and deer out of a last century Gaelic poem about Oisin's journey to the country of the young. After the hunting of the hornless deer, that leads him to the seashore, and while he is riding over the sea with Niam, he sees amid the waters—I have not the Gaelic poem by me, and describe it from memory—a young man following a girl who has a golden apple, and afterwards a hound with one red ear following a deer with no horns. This hound and this deer seem plain images of the desire of man 'which is for the woman,' and 'the desire of the woman which is for the desire of the man,' and of all desires that are as these. I have read them in this way in 'The Wanderings of Usheen' or Oisin, and have made my lover sigh because he has seen in their faces 'the immortal desire of immortals.' A solar mythologist would perhaps say that the girl with the golden apple was once the winter, or night, carrying the sun away, and the deer without horns, like the boar without bristles, darkness flying the light. He would certainly, I think, say that when Cuchullain, whom Professor Rhys calls a solar hero, hunted the enchanted deer of Slieve Fuadh, because the battle fury was still on him, he was the sun pursuing clouds, or cold, or darkness. I have understood them in this sense in 'Hanrahan laments because of his wandering,' and made Hanrahan long for the day when they, fragments of ancestral darkness, will overthrow the world. The desire of the woman, the flying darkness, it is all one! The image—a cross, a man preaching in the wilderness, a dancing Salome, a lily in a girl's hand, a flame leaping, a globe with wings, a pale sunset over still waters—is an eternal act; but our understandings are temporal and understand but a little at a time.

The man in my poem who has a hazel wand may have been Aengus, Master of Love; and I have made the boar without bristles come out of the West, because the place of sunset was in Ireland, as in other countries, a place of symbolic darkness and death.

THE CAP AND BELLS.

I dreamed this story exactly as I have written it, and dreamed another long dream after it, trying to make out its meaning, and whether I was to write it in prose or verse. The first dream was more a vision than a dream, for it was beautiful and coherent, and gave me the sense of illumination and exaltation that one gets from visions, while the second dream was confused and meaningless. The poem has always meant a great deal to me, though, as is the way with symbolic poems, it has not always meant quite the same thing. Blake would have said 'the authors are in eternity,' and I am quite sure they can only be questioned in dreams.

THE VALLEY OF THE BLACK PIG.

All over Ireland there are prophecies of the coming rout of the enemies of Ireland, in a certain Valley of the Black Pig, and these prophecies are, no doubt, now, as they were in the Fenian days, a political force. I have heard of one man who would not give any money to the Land League, because the Battle could not be until the close of the century; but, as a rule, periods of trouble bring prophecies of its near coming. A few years before my time, an old man who lived at Lisadell, in Sligo, used to fall down in a fit and rave out descriptions of the Battle; and a man in Sligo has told me that it will be so great a battle that the horses shall go up to their fetlocks in blood, and that their girths, when it is over, will rot from their bellies for lack of a hand to unbuckle them. The battle is a mythological battle, and the black pig is one with the bristleless boar, that killed Dearmod, in November, upon the western end of Ben Bulben; Misroide MacDatha's sow, whose carving brought on so great a battle; 'the croppy black sow,' and 'the cutty black sow' of Welsh November rhymes ('Celtic Heathendom,' pages 509-516); the boar that killed Adonis; the boar that killed Attis; and the pig embodiment of Typhon ('Golden Bough,' II. pages 26, 31). The pig seems to have been originally a genius of the corn, and, seemingly because the too great power of their divinity makes divine things dangerous to mortals, its flesh was forbidden to many eastern nations; but as the meaning of the prohibition was forgotten, abhorrence took the place of reverence, pigs and boars grew into types of evil, and were described as the enemies of the very gods they once typified ('Golden Bough,' II. 26-31, 56-57). The Pig would, therefore, become the Black Pig, a type of cold and of winter that awake in November, the old beginning of winter, to do battle with the summer, and with the fruit and leaves, and finally, as I suggest; and as I believe, for the purposes of poetry; of the darkness that will at last destroy the gods and the world. The country people say there is no shape for a spirit to take so dangerous as the shape of a pig; and a Galway blacksmith—and blacksmiths are thought to be especially protected—says he would be afraid to meet a pig on the road at night; and another Galway man tells this story: 'There was a man coming the road from Gort to Garryland one night, and he had a drop taken; and before him, on the road, he saw a pig walking; and having a drop in, he gave a shout, and made a kick at it, and bid it get out of that. And by the time he got home, his arm was swelled from the shoulder to be as big as a bag, and he couldn't use his hand with the pain of it. And his wife brought him, after a few days, to a woman that used to do cures at Rahasane. And on the road all she could do would hardly keep him from lying down to sleep on the grass. And when they got to the woman she knew all that happened; and, says she, it's well for you that your wife didn't let you fall asleep on the grass, for if you had done that but even for one instant, you'd be a lost man.'

It is possible that bristles were associated with fertility, as the tail certainly was, for a pig's tail is stuck into the ground in Courland, that the corn may grow abundantly, and the tails of pigs, and other animal embodiments of the corn genius, are dragged over the ground to make it fertile in different countries. Professor Rhys, who considers the bristleless boar a symbol of darkness and cold, rather than of winter and cold, thinks it was without bristles because the darkness is shorn away by the sun. It may have had different meanings, just as the scourging of the man-god has had different though not contradictory meanings in different epochs of the world.

The Battle should, I believe, be compared with three other battles; a battle the Sidhe are said to fight when a person is being taken away by them; a battle they are said to fight in November for the harvest; the great battle the Tribes of the goddess Danu fought, according to the Gaelic chroniclers, with the Fomor at Moy Tura, or the Towery Plain.

I have heard of the battle over the dying both in County Galway and in the Isles of Arann, an old Arann fisherman having told me that it was fought over two of his children, and that he found blood in a box he had for keeping fish, when it was over; and I have written about it, and given examples elsewhere. A faery doctor, on the borders of Galway and Clare, explained it as a battle between the friends and enemies of the dying, the one party trying to take them, the other trying to save them from being taken. It may once, when the land of the Sidhe was the only other world, and when every man who died was carried thither, have always accompanied death. I suggest that the battle between the Tribes of the goddess Danu, the powers of light, and warmth, and fruitfulness, and goodness, and the Fomor, the powers of darkness, and cold, and barrenness, and badness upon the Towery Plain, was the establishment of the habitable world, the rout of the ancestral darkness; that the battle among the Sidhe for the harvest is the annual battle of summer and winter; that the battle among the Sidhe at a man's death is the battle of life and death; and that the battle of the Black Pig is the battle between the manifest world and the ancestral darkness at the end of all things; and that all these battles are one, the battle of all things with shadowy decay. Once a symbolism has possessed the imagination of large numbers of men, it becomes, as I believe, an embodiment of disembodied powers, and repeats itself in dreams and visions, age after age.

THE SECRET ROSE.

I find that I have unintentionally changed the old story of Conchobar's death. He did not see the crucifixion in a vision, but was told about it. He had been struck by a ball, made of the dried brain of a dead enemy, and hurled out of a sling; and this ball had been left in his head, and his head had been mended, the Book of Leinster says, with thread of gold because his hair was like gold. Keating, a writer of the time of Elizabeth, says, 'In that state did he remain seven years, until the Friday on which Christ was crucified, according to some historians; and when he saw the unusual changes of the creation and the eclipse of the sun and the moon at its full, he asked of Bucrach, a Leinster Druid, who was along with him, what was it that brought that unusual change upon the planets of Heaven and Earth. "Jesus Christ, the son of God," said the Druid, "who is now being crucified by the Jews." "That is a pity," said Conchobar; "were I in his presence I would kill those who were putting him to death." And with that he brought out his sword, and rushed at a woody grove which was convenient to him, and began to cut and fell it; and what he said was, that if he were among the Jews that was the usage he would give them, and from the excessiveness of his fury which seized upon him, the ball started out of his head, and some of the brain came after it, and in that way he died. The wood of Lanshraigh, in Feara Rois, is the name by which that shrubby wood is called.'

I have imagined Cuchullain meeting Fand 'walking among flaming dew.' The story of their love is one of the most beautiful of our old tales. Two birds, bound one to another with a chain of gold, came to a lake side where Cuchullain and the host of Uladh was encamped, and sang so sweetly that all the host fell into a magic sleep. Presently they took the shape of two beautiful women, and cast a magical weakness upon Cuchullain, in which he lay for a year. At the year's end an Aengus, who was probably Aengus the master of love, one of the greatest of the children of the goddess Danu, came and sat upon his bedside, and sang how Fand, the wife of Mannannan, the master of the sea, and of the islands of the dead, loved him; and that if he would come into the country of the gods, where there was wine and gold and silver, Fand, and Laban her sister, would heal him of his magical weakness. Cuchullain went to the country of the gods, and, after being for a month the lover of Fand, made her a promise to meet her at a place called 'the Yew at the Strand's End,' and came back to the earth. Emer, his mortal wife, won his love again, and Mannannan came to 'the Yew at the Strand's End,' and carried Fand away. When Cuchullain saw her going, his love for her fell upon him again, and he went mad, and wandered among the mountains without food or drink, until he was at last cured by a Druid drink of forgetfulness.

I have founded the man 'who drove the gods out of their Liss,' or fort, upon something I have read about Caolte after the battle of Gabra, when almost all his companions were killed, driving the gods out of their Liss, either at Osraighe, now Ossory, or at Eas Ruaidh, now Asseroe, a waterfall at Ballyshannon, where Ilbreac, one of the children of the goddess Danu, had a Liss. I am writing away from most of my books, and have not been able to find the passage; but I certainly read it somewhere.

I have founded 'the proud dreaming king' upon Fergus, the son of Roigh, the legendary poet of 'the quest of the bull of Cualge,' as he is in the ancient story of Deirdre, and in modern poems by Ferguson. He married Nessa, and Ferguson makes him tell how she took him 'captive in a single look.'

'I am but an empty shade,
Far from life and passion laid;
Yet does sweet remembrance thrill
All my shadowy being still.'

Presently, because of his great love, he gave up his throne to Conchobar, her son by another, and lived out his days feasting, and fighting, and hunting. His promise never to refuse a feast from a certain comrade, and the mischief that came by his promise, and the vengeance he took afterwards, are a principal theme of the poets. I have explained my imagination of him in 'Fergus and the Druid,' and in a little song in the second act of 'The Countess Kathleen.'

I have founded him 'who sold tillage, and house, and goods,' upon something in 'The Red Pony,' a folk tale in Mr. Larminie's 'West Irish Folk Tales.' A young man 'saw a light before him on the high road. When he came as far, there was an open box on the road, and a light coming up out of it. He took up the box. There was a lock of hair in it. Presently he had to go to become the servant of a king for his living. There were eleven boys. When they were going out into the stable at ten o'clock, each of them took a light but he. He took no candle at all with him. Each of them went into his own stable. When he went into his stable he opened the box. He left it in a hole in the wall. The light was great. It was twice as much as in the other stables.' The king hears of it, and makes him show him the box. The king says, 'You must go and bring me the woman to whom the hair belongs.' In the end, the young man, and not the king, marries the woman.